THE TALE OF

PIP & SQUEAK

Kate Duke

Dutton Children's Books

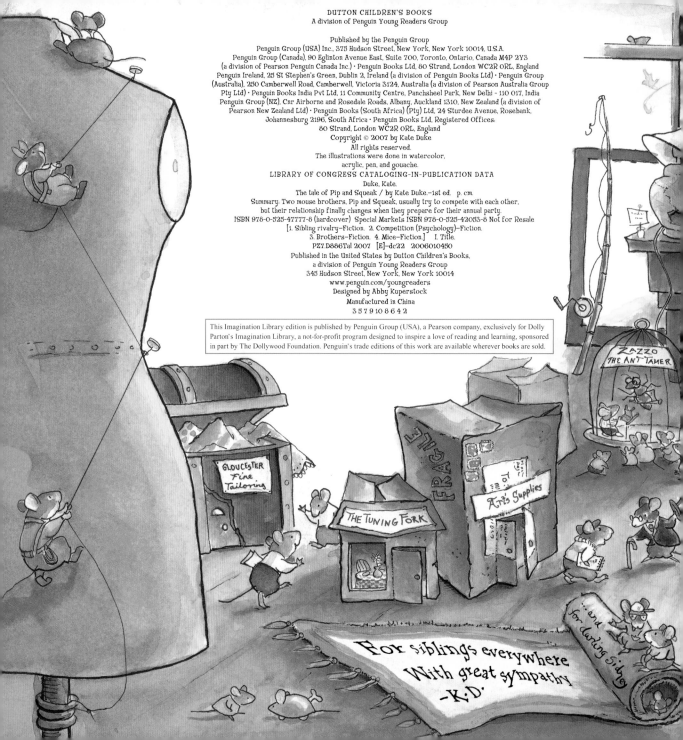

DUTTON CHILDREN'S BOOKS
A division of Penguin Young Readers Group

Published by the Penguin Group
Penguin Group (USA) Inc., 375 Hudson Street, New York, New York 10014, U.S.A.
Penguin Group (Canada), 90 Eglinton Avenue East, Suite 700, Toronto, Ontario, Canada M4P 2Y3
(a division of Pearson Penguin Canada Inc.) · Penguin Books Ltd, 80 Strand, London WC2R ORL, England
Penguin Ireland, 25 St Stephen's Green, Dublin 2, Ireland (a division of Penguin Books Ltd) · Penguin Group
(Australia), 250 Camberwell Road, Camberwell, Victoria 3124, Australia (a division of Pearson Australia Group
Pty Ltd) · Penguin Books India Pvt Ltd, 11 Community Centre, Panchsheel Park, New Delhi - 110 017, India
Penguin Group (NZ), Cnr Airborne and Rosedale Roads, Albany, Auckland 1310, New Zealand (a division of
Pearson New Zealand Ltd) · Penguin Books (South Africa) (Pty) Ltd, 24 Sturdee Avenue, Rosebank,
Johannesburg 2196, South Africa · Penguin Books Ltd, Registered Offices:
80 Strand, London WC2R ORL, England

The illustrations were done in watercolor,
acrylic, pen, and gouache.

LIBRARY OF CONGRESS CATALOGING-IN-PUBLICATION DATA
Duke, Kate.
The tale of Pip and Squeak / by Kate Duke.—1st ed. p. cm.
Summary: Two mouse brothers, Pip and Squeak, usually try to compete with each other,
but their relationship finally changes when they prepare for their annual party.
ISBN 978-0-525-47777-8 (hardcover) Special Markets ISBN 978-0-525-42053-8 Not for Resale
[1. Sibling rivalry–Fiction. 2. Competition (Psychology)–Fiction.
3. Brothers–Fiction. 4. Mice–Fiction.]   I. Title.
PZ7.D886Tal 2007 [E]–dc22 2006010450
Published in the United States by Dutton Children's Books,
a division of Penguin Young Readers Group
345 Hudson Street, New York, New York 10014
www.penguin.com/youngreaders
Designed by Abby Kuperstock
Manufactured in China
3 5 7 9 10 8 6 4 2

This Imagination Library edition is published by Penguin Group (USA), a Pearson company, exclusively for Dolly
Parton's Imagination Library, a not-for-profit program designed to inspire a love of reading and learning, sponsored
in part by The Dollywood Foundation. Penguin's trade editions of this work are available wherever books are sold.

GLOUCESTER
Fine
Tailoring

THE TUNING FORK

FRAGILE

Art's Supplies

ZAZZO
THE ANT TAMER

For siblings everywhere
With great sympathy
–K.D.

...and for darling siblings

Once upon a time . . .

there were two brothers, Pip and Squeak.
They lived together in a big house in a pleasant neighborhood.

Pip was an artist. He painted pictures.

Squeak wrote songs and sang them in a hearty baritone.

Squeak and Pip had lots of friends, but they were not friends with each other.

Pip said the sound of Squeak's singing hurt his ears.

Squeak said the smell of Pip's paint irritated his delicate throat and made him cough so much it was a miracle he could utter a note.

So Pip stayed in his studio
at one end of the house,
and Squeak stayed in his music
room at the other end.

And the very big room in the
middle stayed empty,
except for one day every year.

My side's going to be cleaner than yours!

On that one day, Pip and Squeak
always gave a big party
for all their friends.
The brothers would work
for days getting ready.
They cleaned,
they shopped,
they baked,
they decorated.

These look much better than yours!

My cart is faster than yours!

Green and orange will look nice!

Not as nice as blue and purple!

Squeak always made his special recipe for Hogberry Nog.
And Pip always made HIS special recipe for Hogberry Nog.
Squeak said his was the best in the universe.
Pip said his was the best in the universe plus fifty miles outside it.

Every year the party was the same.
For entertainment, Squeak would sing
his newest songs up in his music room.
Pip stayed downstairs.

Then Pip would show off
his latest paintings up in his studio.
Squeak stayed downstairs.

But one year, something new happened.
Squeak wrote a very long song.
It was his longest song ever.
"I'm going to sing it in the
big room," he told Pip,

"and I'll stand on
a real stage,

and I'll be the star
of the party!"

"No fair!" cried Pip.

He ran upstairs
and started painting some new pictures.

They were his biggest pictures ever.
Soon there was no more room for them in the studio.

Downstairs in the big room, though, there was plenty of space.
"Hey!" shouted Squeak. "You've ruined my stage! This is a mess!"
"It is not," said Pip. "It is my art exhibit. My paintings will
be everywhere, and I'LL be the star of the party!"

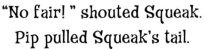"No fair! " shouted Squeak.
Pip pulled Squeak's tail.
Squeak yanked Pip's ears.
Pip ran.
Squeak ran after him.
Back
and forth
and up
and down
and around
and around
they went.

Suddenly
Pip tripped.
Squeak slipped.

Chairs tipped,
pictures flipped,
music ripped.

"EEK!" Squeak squawked.
"YEEK!" Pip yipped.

"OH, GEE!" Squeak peeped.
"YIKES!" yelled Pip.

"HEY, look at me!" Squeak squealed.

"WHOOPEE!" Pip squeaked.

"THIS IS FUN!"

piped Pip.

"LOTS OF FUN!"

sang Squeak.

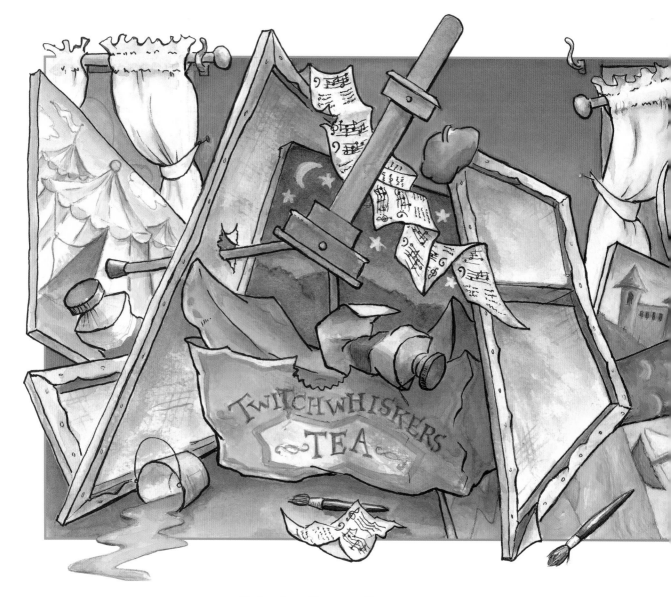

But when it was all over,
the big room was a big mess,
and the brothers were in big trouble—
because the party was the next day.

Together they looked at what they had done.
"I have an idea," said Squeak.
"I have one, too," said Pip.
"I bet mine's better than yours," said Squeak.
But it wasn't. It was the same idea.

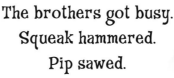

The brothers got busy.
Squeak hammered.
Pip sawed.

Squeak found a curtain.
Pip found a pole.
Squeak noticed a problem.
Pip fixed it.

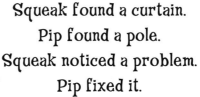

It's too dark!

Pip had to touch up
a few of his pictures.
Squeak watched him,
and he didn't cough once.

Squeak needed
to practice.
Pip stayed and listened,
and his ears felt just fine.

By the night of the party,
everything was ready.

When the curtains parted,
the audience cheered.
Never had Pip's pictures
looked so beautiful or so big.

Never had Squeak sung
so magnificently
or for such a long time.

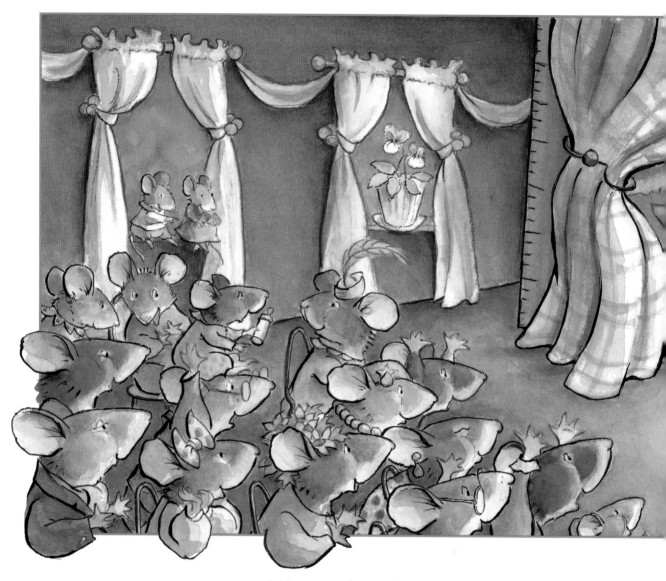

At the end of the show,
Squeak bowed to the audience.
Pip bowed, too.

And then they bowed to each other,
because they were both the stars of the party.
"Bravo, Squeak! Bravo, Pip!" the audience shouted.
"HOORAY! HOORAY!"

The evening was a triumph.

The guests all exclaimed that
this year's party was the most fun ever.
Pip and Squeak had to agree—

although Squeak still said
that his Hogberry Nog
was the best in the universe,

and Pip still said that his
was the best in the universe
plus fifty—no, a hundred—miles outside it.